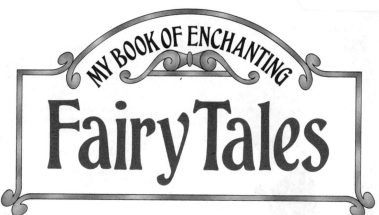

MY BOOK OF ENCHANTING
Fairy Tales

*The stories and illustrations in this book previously
appeared in Gift Book of Hans Christian Andersen
Fairy Tales and Gift Book of Fairy Tales.*

First published 1980 by
Deans International Publishing
under the title *A Gift Book of Enchanting Fairy Tales*

This edition first published in Great Britain 1989 by
Treasure Press
Michelin House
81 Fulham Road
London SW3 6RB

Copyright © Deans International Publishing a division of
The Hamlyn Publishing Group Limited 1970, 1971, 1973, 1974

ISBN 1 85051 416 X

Produced by Mandarin Offset
Printed in Hong Kong

MY BOOK OF ENCHANTING
Fairy Tales

Illustrated by

Janet & Anne Grahame Johnstone

TREASURE PRESS

CONTENTS

LITTLE RED RIDING HOOD

THERE was once a little girl who lived with her father and mother in a cottage on the edge of a great forest.

The girl's father was a woodcutter and every day he went out to fell trees in the forest.

Just inside the forest there was another cottage and here lived the little girl's grandmother, who one day made her granddaughter a lovely riding hood and cloak in the brightest scarlet cloth.

The little girl wore her lovely bright cloak and hood whenever she went out and everybody called her Red Riding Hood.

One morning Red Riding Hood's mother said, "Your grandmother is not very well today, so I have made her a sweet custard and some fresh butter. You may take them to her as a gift, but remember to go straight there and straight back again."

Little Red Riding Hood put on her gay cloak and hood and took the basket from her mother, but she had not gone far down the road towards the forest and her grandmother's cottage when she came upon a great wolf sitting across her path.

"Hello, Red Riding Hood," grinned the wolf. "Where are you off to this fine morning?"

"I am going to see my grandmother who is not very well," replied the little girl. "I have some custard and fresh butter for her."

The wolf smacked his lips, but he was not thinking of the custard and butter. He was thinking that he might be able to make a meal

of Red Riding Hood's grandmother and the little girl herself!

"Does your granny live far away, Red Riding Hood?" asked the wolf.

"Her cottage is just down the forest path," replied the little girl.

"Then I will go and see her as well," said the wolf.

"That is very good of you," said Red Riding Hood. "I am going to gather some flowers for her and then we can walk along together."

But the wicked wolf had other plans.

"Let us see who will get to your granny's cottage first," he said. "I will take *this* path and you can follow *that* one."

Now the wolf had pointed out the longer way to Red Riding Hood. She forgot her mother's words and went off down the path the wolf had shown her. She stopped on the way to gather flowers, and she chased the butterflies while the wolf bounded along his shorter path as quickly as he could.

When the wolf came to the cottage he knocked on the door.

"Who is there?" called the old lady from her bed.

"It is Red Riding Hood!" replied the wolf, trying to sound like a little girl.

"Pull the bobbin and the latch will go up," cried the grandmother.

The wolf did as he was told and then bounded into the room.

When the old lady saw the great wolf with his long red tongue and sharp white teeth, she jumped from her bed and ran out of the back door so quickly that even the wolf couldn't catch her.

He did not chase her but instead he waited for Red Riding Hood. He dressed himself in one of the old lady's nightdresses and put on one of her nightcaps, then slipped into the bed in her place.

When Red Riding Hood at last reached the cottage, she knocked at the door.

"Who is there?" asked the wolf.

"Poor Granny does sound hoarse!" thought the little girl. "It is Red Riding Hood," she cried aloud. "I have brought you a custard and some fresh butter."

"Pull the bobbin and the latch will go up," called the wolf, trying to sound like Granny.

Red Riding Hood went into the cottage, and after taking off her hood and cloak, she sat on her grandmother's bed.

The wolf hid himself as well as he could under the bed covers, but Red Riding Hood noticed his long arms.

"Grandmama, what great arms you have!" she cried with surprise.

"All the better to hug you with, my dear!" said the wolf.

"Grandmama, what great legs you have!" said Red Riding Hood, next.

"All the better to run with, my dear!" cried the wolf.

"Grandmama, what great ears you have!" said Red Riding Hood.

"All the better to hear you with, my dear!" cried the wolf.

"Grandmama, what great eyes you have," said Red Riding Hood, peering at the wolf.

"All the better to see you with, my dear!" grinned the wolf.

"Grandmama, what great teeth you have!" exclaimed little Red Riding Hood.

"All the better to EAT you with, my dear!" snarled the wolf.

Red Riding Hood gave a loud, frightened scream as she jumped off the bed.

The wolf leapt out of the bed, but before he could catch the little girl, the door opened and in hurried her woodcutter father, with his sharp hatchet.

The wicked wolf tore past the woodcutter, out through the doorway, and ran for his life!

Red Riding Hood's grandmother crept back into her cottage when she saw the wolf go, and after hugging the little girl, she got back into her bed.

She thankfully ate the sweet egg custard and the fresh butter that her granddaughter had brought her and felt very much better.

Little Red Riding Hood soon forgot how frightened she had been when she saw her grandmother's smiling face and walked happily through the forest by her father's side, back to their own cottage.

Mother Goose

OLD Mother Goose,
When she wanted to wander,
Would ride through the air
On a very fine gander.

Mother Goose had a house,
'Twas built in a wood.
Where an owl at the door
For a sentinel stood.

She had a son Jack,
A plain looking lad,
He was not very good,
Nor yet very bad.

She sent him to market,
A live goose he bought;
"See, Mother," says he,
"I have not been for nought."

Jack's goose and her gander
Grew very fond;
They'd both eat together,
Or swim in the pond.

Jack found one fine morning,
As I have been told,
His goose had laid him
An egg of pure gold.

Jack ran to his mother
The news for to tell,
She called him a good boy,
And said it was well.

Jack sold his gold egg
To a merchant untrue,
Who cheated him out of
A half of his due.

Then Jack went a-courting
A lady so gay;
As fair as a lily
And sweet as the May.

The merchant and squire
Soon came at his back,
And began to belabour
The sides of poor Jack.

Then old Mother Goose
That instant came in,
And turned her son Jack
Into famed Harlequin.

She then with her wand,
Touched the lady so fine,
And turned her at once
Into sweet Columbine.

The gold egg in the sea
Was thrown away then,
When a mermaid brought
The egg back again.

The merchant then vowed
The goose he would kill,
Resolving at once
His pockets to fill.

Jack's mother came in,
And caught the goose soon,
And mounting its back,
Flew up to the moon.

HOP O' MY THUMB

ONCE upon a time there were seven little boys, all brothers. Hop o' my Thumb was the youngest and smallest of them all.

One day, they followed their father, a woodman, into a wood where they had never been before. The family were very poor and their father worked from sunrise to sunset for money to buy food and clothes for them all.

The boys were all too young to work but they thought they might gather some sticks to sell in the village for firewood.

As they ran deeper into the wood, some of the boys

began to cry, but Hop o' my Thumb told them not to be frightened.

"But we are lost!" sobbed one of the boys.

"Come on," cried Tom, the eldest, "we must find Father."

"Let us gather some sticks," said Hop o' my Thumb, "then we can go home."

"We don't know *how* to get home," said Teddy, the next to youngest.

"*I* do," said Hop o' my Thumb, who had filled all his pockets with pebbles from the banks of a little stream earlier in the day, and

had been dropping them behind him as he
followed his brothers into the wood.

"Oh look, there's a cottage behind the trees," cried
Tom.

"I'll ask them if they can give us a drink of water,"
said Hop o' my Thumb.

The old lady who opened the door said, "Go away, little boy, a fierce
giant lives here and he does not like children. He is counting his gold
under a tree."

At that moment, the giant came running towards them, wearing his
Seven League Boots. The boys took to their heels and fled, while the
giant came striding after them, but Hop o' my Thumb still went on
scattering pebbles as he led his brothers in and out of the trees, trying
to tire the giant out, for the boys were young and thin,
and the giant was old and fat.

"Oh goodness, what shall I do if he catches us?" cried
Tim, the next to eldest.

"He *won't* catch us," promised brave little Hop o' my

Thumb. "Listen I can't hear him crashing through the bushes now, can you?" And all his brothers shook their heads.

"Well," said Hop o' my Thumb, sitting on a log, "I think we have been very lucky indeed."

His six brothers were so tired after their running up and down, and in and out of the woodland trees to try to escape the giant that *they* decided to lie down and have a little nap before following Hop o' my Thumb's pebbles out of the wood.

"It was a wonderful idea," said Tom, "now we can soon get home again."

But while his brothers slept, Hop o' my Thumb kept trying to think of some way of getting money for their mother and father.

In a little while, his brothers wakened up and they all washed their hands and faces in a woodland pool, then, on their way home, they came on the giant fast asleep and snoring, and Hop o' my Thumb had another bright idea.

Very carefully he pulled off one of the sleeping giant's Seven League Boots, and he began to put his foot in it.

To the brothers' surprise, the Seven League Boot grew as tiny as Hop o' my Thumb's own foot and fitted him perfectly, and as soon as he began to put on the other Seven League Boot, that also began to grow smaller.

"They're *magic* boots!" whispered Hop o' my Thumb. "Now I'm going back to the cottage in the wood, and you must come after me as fast as you can, but be very quiet in case the horrid old giant wakes up," and smiling at his brothers he set off as fast as the wind in the Seven League Boots.

The brothers ran after Hop o' my Thumb as quietly as they could, and the giant, who had eaten a huge dinner that day, and as he was fat and lazy, did not awake. He loved sleeping almost as much as he loved his bag of gold.

"I wonder what Hop o' my Thumb is going to do?" said Teddy, the next to youngest brother, as they ran through the wood keeping the pebbles in sight so that they would not lose their way.

When Hop o' my Thumb reached the giant's cottage, he told the housekeeper that the giant wanted his bag of gold at once, and he had lent him his boots to get it quickly. She brought out the bag of gold, and Hop o' my Thumb thanked her and staggered off with it to meet his brothers.

Sitting down under a tree, Hop o' my Thumb waited for them to arrive, and when they did, they could hardly believe their eyes. "You *are* clever, Hop o' my Thumb!" cried Tom. Then Hop o' my Thumb picked up the bag of gold, again!

At home, the boys' mother and father were very, very upset. Their father had turned back to look for them in the wood, but he had somehow missed them. He had hunted for them for hours and had then gone back home, hoping to find them there safe and well.

Their mother cried bitterly and they had told all their neighbours, who said they would search the wood and fields for them when they had finished work.

But it was growing dark before they were ready to start the search, and a mist was rising from the valley.

"Oh dear," sobbed the boys' mother, "we shall never see our dear little sons again!" And then, oh joy! there came the sound of whistling outside the cottage and the tramping of feet. "It's our boys!" cried their mother, and she and their father ran out; their father carrying his lantern.

"Oh, Mother and Father, we are rich!" cried Hop o' my Thumb. "Now we can buy a food farm and we can all help Father with the work!"

GOLDILOCKS AND THE THREE BEARS

IN a pretty little house in a large forest, a long time ago, there lived three bears. Father Bear, Mother Bear and Baby Bear.

One day the bears' breakfast porridge was so hot that they went for a walk while it cooled. At the same time a little girl named Goldilocks went for a walk, also, and she saw the house.

Goldilocks peeped through the keyhole, but could not see very much, which made her all the more curious to see what was inside the tiny house, and she wondered who could live there.

Goldilocks looked through the little window and could see that no one was at home, so she went to the door and tried the handle. To her great surprise the door opened, so she walked into the house.

The first room she entered was the bears' dining-room. On the table she saw three bowls of porridge; one was very large, the second was a little smaller, and the third a very tiny one, and as she felt hungry after her long walk, she thought she would try the porridge.

First she tried the large bowl, but the porridge was too hot. Then she tried the second; "This porridge has gone quite cold!" she said. "I do not like it!"

There was only the tiny wee bowl left and Goldilocks filled the little spoon with porridge and popped it into her mouth. The porridge in this bowl was so exactly right that Goldilocks ate up every scrap!

After that she felt tired and so she went to the great big chair to sit down on it, but it was too big and the cushion was too hard for her.

Next Goldilocks tried the middle-sized chair, but this one was so soft that the little girl almost got lost in it.

That left the tiny wee chair and Goldilocks went and sat down on it. This was just the right size for Goldilocks but alas! *she* was not the right size for *it!* CRACK! one of the legs snapped off and the little girl fell to the floor.

"I *must* have a rest," decided Goldilocks. "I will go upstairs and see if the beds are any better than the chairs."

She climbed up the stairs and went to the first bed, which was the great big one.

Goldilocks tried to climb up on to it, but it was so high up that she could not manage it.

"I will try the smaller bed," she said.

Goldilocks went to the middle-sized bed. She got into this one quite

easily, but it was far too soft and warm and the little girl did not like it.

"I will try the tiny bed," sighed Goldilocks.

She went to the tiny wee bed and climbed inside it, then she pulled the pretty quilt over herself and curled up happily.

"This bed is just right!" she murmured, and she went off to sleep.

In the meantime, the bears had finished their walk and they turned to go home to eat up their porridge.

When they came to their little house, they found the door wide open. Father Bear went up to his great big bowl of porridge.

"Someone has been eating MY porridge!" he roared.

Mother Bear went and looked at her middle-sized bowl.

"Someone has been eating MY porridge!" she growled.

Baby Bear hurried to his tiny wee bowl.

"Someone has been tasting MY porridge!" he squealed. "And they have eaten it all up!"

Then Father Bear saw that the cushion in his chair had been moved.

"Someone has been sitting on MY chair!" he roared.

Mother Bear went to her middle-sized chair, and saw that the seat was rumpled.

"Someone has been sitting on MY chair!" she growled.

Baby Bear ran to his tiny wee chair.

"Someone has been sitting on MY chair!" he squeaked. "And they have broken it!"

Father Bear was now very angry indeed. He picked up the little

chair to see if he could mend it, but he quickly put it down again, saying: "We must look all over the house in case anyone is still here!"

The three bears peered into every corner of the dining-room and the kitchen, but they could not find anyone, so they climbed up the stairs to the bedroom.

Father Bear went to his great big bed and saw that the cover was crumpled.

"Someone has been sleeping in MY bed!" he roared.

Mother Bear hurried to her middle-sized bed and saw the creased patchwork quilt.

"Someone has been sleeping in MY bed!" she growled.

Baby Bear ran to his tiny wee bed and saw that there was something under his quilt. He looked closer, and there was Goldilocks fast asleep, cuddling one of his toys.

"Someone has been sleeping in MY bed!" he squealed. "AND HERE SHE IS!"

At the sound of Baby Bear's loud, squeaky voice, Goldilocks awakened with a start.

She quickly sat up and stared at the tiny wee Baby Bear and he stared back at her.

Goldilocks, knowing she should not be there, jumped out of the bed and ran down the stairs and out of the little house as fast as she could.

The three bears went after her, but she ran so quickly that they could not have caught her if they had tried, so they went back into their little house and closed the door.

Mother Bear went upstairs to tidy the beds, then she hurried downstairs to start making some fresh porridge, for they were all very hungry by now.

Father Bear was busy too, he made a new leg for Baby Bear's chair so that it was as good as new.

Baby Bear, however, just stood looking out of the window. He was feeling rather sad for he thought Goldilocks was beautiful and he would have liked her for a playmate.

THE THREE LITTLE PIGS

Once upon a time there were three little pigs. When they grew big enough to look after themselves, the first little pig decided to leave his mother and two brothers and go out into the world.

"The world is a dangerous place," said his mother. "The first thing you should do is build yourself a house and then you will be safe inside it."

"That is a very good idea," said the first little pig. "I am a wise little pig. I will soon make my way in the world and become a well-to-do grown-up pig."

The little pig's brothers thought he was very brave and they did all they could to help him get ready for his journey.

The first little pig dressed himself in his best clothes and put his toothbrush and his other important things in the middle of a big red and white spotted handkerchief and then he tied the corners together over a stick, so that he could carry it over his shoulder.

Then the first little pig put on a shady hat and kissed his mother goodbye.

"You can all come and stay with me when I am a rich pig in a home of my own," he promised.

"Look out for wicked wolves," his mother warned.

The other little pigs trotted across the fields with their brother until they came to the wide open road which led out into the world.

"Which way are you going?" asked the second little pig.

The first little pig thought for a long time and then he pointed along the road where it stretched over the hills and far away.

"I shall go that way," he said.

So the first little pig trotted away down the road, waving to his brothers until they could not see him any more.

The first little pig strode along bravely, feeling very pleased with himself. But he was not used to walking such a long way and he soon began to feel tired.

When he saw a man coming along with a great truss of straw on his back, the little pig decided that already the time had come to build himself a house to live in.

The little pig stopped in front of the man and spoke very politely.

"Please, sir, will you be so good as to give me some straw to build myself a house?" he asked.

The man was so pleased to meet a little pig with such good manners that he smiled down at him and said:

"I already have as much straw as I want for my new home. You can have all this bundle for your house."

The first little pig was delighted. He began at once to twist and weave and shape the straw, and he worked so hard that before long he had finished his little straw house. He made himself a chair and a little round table, then he sat down to have his supper.

"It has not taken me long to get settled down in a beautiful new house!" cried the first little pig, proudly. "Soon I shall be able to invite my two brothers to stay with me!"

Now the little pig was not as wise as he thought, or he would have known that it was not a very good idea to build a house of straw, and he should have looked around for something much stronger.

In the meantime, the second little pig had decided that the time had come for him to leave home and follow his brother out into the world. "Take care," warned his mother. "The world is a dangerous place."

"I will build myself a house and you can come and stay with me," said the second little pig.

So he put on his best clothes and found a walking stick on which to tie his bundle.

Then he filled a red and white spotted handkerchief with all the things he would need and then kissed his mother goodbye.

Once again the third little pig went with him across the fields to the same wide road which led out into the world.

The third little pig waved farewell to his second brother and then went back home to keep his mother company.

As for the second little pig, he had not gone far before he felt as tired as his brother had done. He was very pleased to see a man coming towards him carrying a great bundle of sticks.

"Those sticks are just what I want to build myself a new home," said the little pig to the man. "Would you be so kind as to let me have some of them?"

The man liked the polite little pig so much that he gave him a great bundle of them.

At once the second pig started to build his house and before very long it was all ready for him to live in.

Now the third little pig felt lonely without his brothers and he decided to follow them out into the world. He put on his best clothes and packed his things in a little case and then he kissed his mother goodbye. "I will build myself a house so that you can come and live with me," he told her.

He trotted across the fields until he came to the wide road and then he walked along it, just as his brothers had done before him.

The third little pig had not gone far before he met a man with a load of bricks. "Ho! ho! Those bricks would make me a good strong house!" said the wise little pig.

He went up to the man and asked so politely for some bricks that the man was glad to give him enough to build a lovely little house.

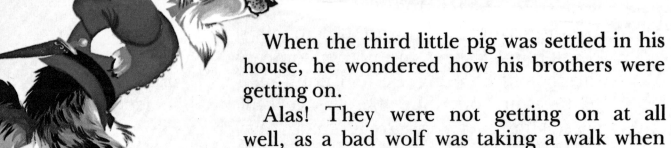

When the third little pig was settled in his house, he wondered how his brothers were getting on.

Alas! They were not getting on at all well, as a bad wolf was taking a walk when he came upon the first little pig's straw house.

"I do not remember seeing that before," he said to himself, and he padded up to the straw walls and sniffed all round them.

"I wonder who lives in this dear little house?" thought the wolf, slyly licking his lips.

He gave a delighted grin. He could smell the little pig who was sitting inside thinking he was settled for life, without a care in the world.

"Little pig, little pig, let me come in!" cried the wolf.

But the little pig knew the wolf's voice and he remembered what his mother had said.

"No, no, by the hair on my chinny-chin-chin!" squeaked the little pig, boldly.

"Then I'll huff and I'll puff and I'll blow your house down!" snarled the wolf.

So the wolf huffed and he puffed until the house of straw blew away and the little pig had to run away as fast as he could to save himself from the wolf.

The wolf was very cross and he went on walking until he came to the second pig's little house. "I see another new house," said the wolf. "I wonder who lives in this one?" He sniffed around the walls, and under the door he could smell the little pig.

"Little pig, little pig, let me come in!" he cried.

But the second little pig could see the wolf's ears through the door.

"No, no, by the hair on my chinny-chin-chin!" he squealed.

"Then I'll huff and I'll puff and I'll blow your house down!" growled the wolf. And he huffed and he puffed until he blew down the house made of sticks and the little pig had to run for his life!

He had been just as unwise as his brother by building a house which could easily be blown away.

The wolf was very hungry now and when he came to the third little house he smelled pig again, and he felt sure that today he would catch this one for his meal after he had blown down the house.

"Open the door, little pig!" snarled the wolf. But the third little pig saw the wolf's paws through a crack in the door.

"No, no, by the hair on my chinny-chin-chin!" he cried.

"Then I'll huff and I'll puff and I'll blow your house down!" snapped the wolf. So he huffed and he puffed and he PUFFED and he HUFFED but he could *not* blow down the house.

At last the wolf said, "Little pig, little pig, I can tell you where there are some nice juicy turnips."

"Where are they?" asked the little pig.

"In the field at the top of the lane," grinned the wolf. "If you will be ready at six o'clock in the morning I will take you to get some for your dinner."

"I will be ready," said the little pig. But the next morning he got up at five o'clock and ran to the field. He found the turnips and took some home for his dinner.

At six o'clock the cunning wolf knocked at the door.

"I am waiting, little pig!" he cried.

"Please don't wait any longer," cried the little pig. "My turnips are already cooking for dinner."

The wolf was very angry. "Little pig, little pig," he cried again. "I know where there are some fine apples!"

"Where are they?" asked the little pig.

"On a tree at the bottom of the lane," replied the wolf. "If you will be ready at five o'clock I will take you there."

"I will be ready," said the little pig. But he got up at four o'clock and hurried to the apple tree. He climbed the tree and picked some apples and was just going to climb down when the wolf arrived.

"You did not wait for me, little pig," grinned the wolf.

"N-no, I was so hungry," said the little pig. "I will throw you an apple." He threw the apple as far away as he could and the silly wolf ran after it. The clever little pig scrambled down from the tree and ran away home.

The next day the wolf knocked at the door again. "Will you come to the Fair with me, little pig?" he pleaded. "I will call for you at three o'clock."

As usual, the little pig started off before the wolf came. He enjoyed the Fair and bought a big butter churn. He was late going home, and on the way he saw the wolf coming up the hill towards him.

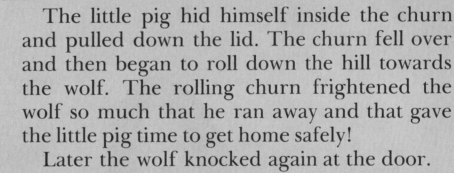

The little pig hid himself inside the churn and pulled down the lid. The churn fell over and then began to roll down the hill towards the wolf. The rolling churn frightened the wolf so much that he ran away and that gave the little pig time to get home safely!

Later the wolf knocked again at the door.

"A great thing chased me away from the Fair," he said.

"That was my new butter churn," chortled the little pig. "And *I* was inside it!" When he heard that the wolf was so angry that he decided to climb down the chimney of the brick house.

But the third little pig was much too clever for the wolf. As soon as he heard the wolf on the roof, he put a large cauldron of water on the fire. The wolf climbed into the chimney, and slid down. And SPLASH! He fell right into the cauldron of water.

By this time the other two little pigs had arrived and were just going to help their brother when the wolf managed to scramble out of the cauldron and ran off into the woods—never to return.

Then the three little pigs settled down happily together in their safe little brick house.

RUMPELSTILTSKIN

THERE was once a poor miller who had a daughter. One day he had to go inside the King's palace on business. He was so pleased at this honour that he tried to make himself into somebody much more important than he really was.

He told the King that he had a beautiful daughter who could spin gold out of straw!

"You may bring her to see me," the King told the miller, who was already beginning to regret his boasting. "I would like her to do some of this wonderful spinning for me."

The next day the frightened miller took his poor daughter to visit the King. The King was delighted to see that she was indeed beautiful. He led the girl to a small room and when he opened the door she saw that it was full from floor to ceiling with straw!

The King pointed to the spinning wheel. "Set to work and spin until dawn," he told the poor girl.

The miller's daughter had no idea how to spin straw into gold and all she could do was sit and weep.

Suddenly the door opened wide and in peeped a tiny man.

"Why are you crying?" he asked.

"I must spin all this straw into gold by dawn," she wept, "and I do not know how to do it."

"Do not worry about that!" cried the little

man. "I will help you but, first, what will you give me if I do?"

"I will give you my ring," said the girl. She gave it to him, then he sat down at the spinning wheel. It began to turn and twist. The little man fed straw on to the whirring bobbin and the more he put there the more golden coins fell on to the floor.

When dawn came there was no straw left and the room was full of gold!

When the King came to see the girl, he could hardly believe his eyes. He was so pleased that he had another room prepared. This time it was an even bigger room and there was still more straw in it.

"Spin more gold for me, my dear!" cried the King. He shut the door, leaving the poor girl alone with the straw and the spinning wheel.

She did not know what she was going to do without the little man's help and began to cry. The door opened a crack and he peeped round at her once more.

"What will you give me this time if I spin the straw into gold for you?" he asked.

"I will give you my necklace," cried the girl happily.

The little man took the necklace, then he

sat down at the spinning wheel. Whirr, twist and twirl went the wheel. The bobbin caught in the straw and cast it out again in the shape of hundreds of golden coins, just as it had done before.

When dawn broke all the straw had gone and the room was full of glittering gold!

This time the King was so overjoyed that he had a still larger room filled with straw, which was tightly stacked from floor to ceiling.

"If you spin all this straw into gold I will make you my Queen!" he cried to the miller's daughter.

The girl knew that she could not do it without the little man's help and waited hopefully for him to appear. Sure enough he came!

"What will you give me *this* time if I spin the straw into gold?" he asked.

"Alas, I have nothing to give," wailed the girl.

"Then promise me that when you are Queen you will give me your first son!" demanded the little man.

The girl could do nothing else but promise and at once the little man seated himself at the spinning wheel and began to spin.

The wheel whirred until the room was full of gold, then the sun shone in through the window and the little man went away.

The rich King kept his promise and he made the miller's daughter his Queen.

A year later a son was born to the Queen and she was so happy that she forgot all about the little man and her promise to him until, one day, he appeared in her room and pointed to her baby.

"Give me the child as you promised!" he cried.

The Queen begged him to take anything except her baby and, as he felt rather sorry for her, he told her that if she could guess his name within three days, she could keep her son.

The Queen tried all the names she knew, but she could not guess the little man's name and he went away. He came the next day and she tried with hundreds more, but the little man's name was not one of them.

Before the third day dawned the poor Queen sent a messenger all

over the land to bring back all the strange names he could find, but there were none left.

"But I did see one strange thing," he told the Queen. I was passing a little house with a tiny man dancing and jumping round a fire burning in front of it. He was singing a song and this is what he sang:

"Tomorrow I brew, today I
    bake,
 And then the child away I'll
    take;
 For little deems my royal
    dame
 That Rumpelstiltskin is my
    name!"

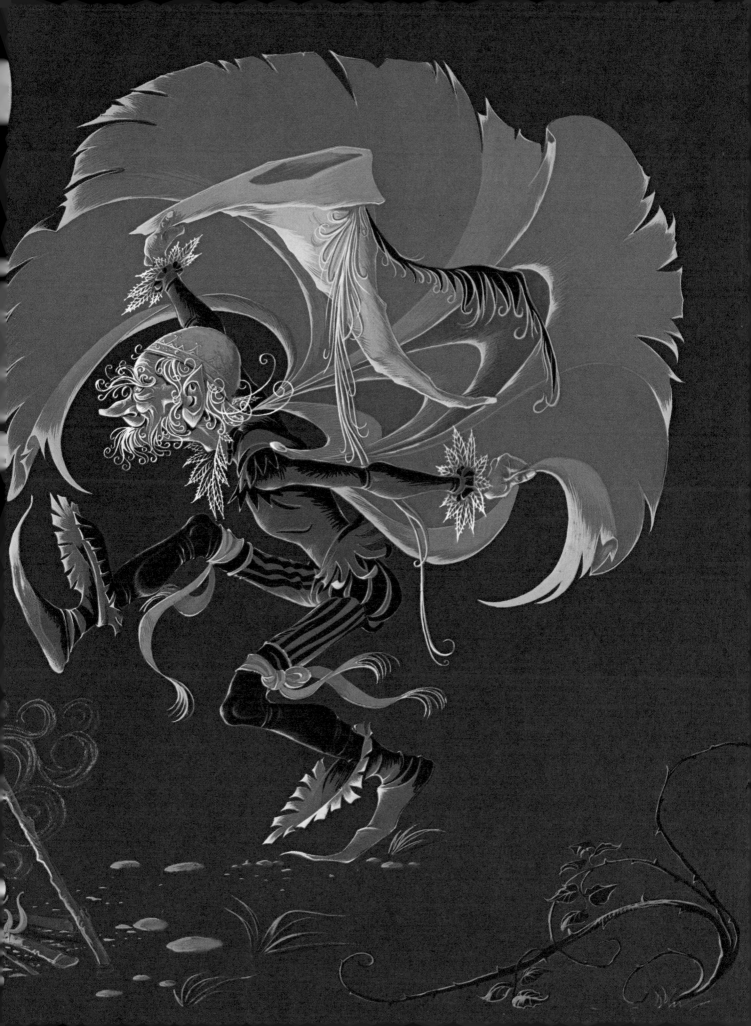

The Queen was delighted to hear this strange name and was very happy when the little man came next time.

She waited for him to speak before she asked him about it, and teased him a little before she said the name her messenger had told her.

"Now, dear lady, what is my name?" asked her visitor.

"Is it Harry?" she asked.

"No!" laughed the little man.

"Is your name Conrad?" she asked.

"No, no!" cried the little man.

"Is your name Timothy?"

"No, no, *no*!" shouted the little man.

"Then your name is Rumpelstiltskin!" said the Queen.

"Some witch told you that! Some witch told you that!" cried the little man, and he was so angry that he stamped his foot so hard he sank right down into the ground out of sight and never troubled the Queen again.

JACK AND THE BEANSTALK

ONCE upon a time there lived a poor widow who had a son, named Jack. One day they found there was nothing left for them to do but to sell their cow to get some money to buy food and keep themselves alive.

Neither the widow nor her son wanted to do this as they were very fond of the animal, but there was nothing else to do and so Jack set off early to walk the cow to market.

Before he came to the town, however, he met an old man who had a handful of brightly coloured beans which he showed to Jack.

"These are magic beans," he said. "I will give them to you in exchange for the cow."

Now Jack was only a small boy and thought the beans were wonderful. He forgot how much he and his mother needed the

money he could get for the animal and he took the beans.

"The cow is yours!" he cried.

The man smiled. "You will not regret having sold the cow to me for the beans," he said. "Good luck to you, my lad." And he went on his way, leading the cow.

Jack was very excited and ran home as fast as he could to show his mother the lovely beans.

But when he gave them to her he was amazed that she was so angry.

The poor widow wept bitterly and said, between her sobs, "Now we shall starve. These beans are useless. Why haven't you more sense?"

Jack realised how foolish he had been. But what was done could not be changed.

Sadly, he went into the garden.

"The best thing I can do with these is to plant them," he thought.

When he had planted the beans carefully, he returned to the cottage. "I am very sorry, Mother," he said. But the poor woman was still very cross.

"Eat your supper and go straight to bed," she cried.

They ate in silence. This was the last meal they could hope for, now they had no cow.

After supper, Jack helped his mother to clear the table and wash up.

"Now off to bed at once, Jack," said his mother, but she was not quite so cross.

Poor Jack could not get to sleep for a long time. He twisted and turned in his little bed, thinking how stupid he had been.

But at last he fell asleep, and awakened very early the next morning.

When he sat up in bed, he was amazed to see huge leaves coming through his bedroom window. The beans had already grown into a great beanstalk.

Jack hurriedly dressed and ran downstairs, and out into the garden. The beanstalk had climbed up and up until the top of it was out of sight, and the huge leaves almost covered the high cliff which had always towered over the little cottage.

Jack and his mother stared up into the leaves and wondered where the great beanstalk ended.

"I am going to climb up and see!" cried Jack.

With his mother calling to him to be careful Jack climbed up the twisted stems and out of sight. He climbed

bravely towards the sky until he was very tired but still he had not reached the top. He made one last spurt and then he found himself looking over the topmost leaves of the plant and gazing out on wonderful green countryside.

Green fields stretched away to meet soft green woods and forests and at the end of a wide path facing him, Jack could see a fine castle.

He was just about to go and explore when an old lady appeared at his side.

Jack thought the castle might be her home, but when he asked her if she lived there she said she did not but she would tell him the true story of the castle.

"A giant lives there with his wife," said the old lady. "They stole the castle from a brave knight and killed him and his family. Fortunately for her his wife was away from home with their baby son and so she escaped. She still lives at the foot of this green country in a tiny cottage, trying to keep herself and her son. *You* are that son, Jack, and the wife of the brave knight is your poor mother!"

Jack could hardly believe his ears when he heard this story and he wanted to go off at once and fight the giant to regain his father's castle.

"That is good," said the old lady. "Try to get the hen that lays the golden eggs and the harp that talks."

Jack strode boldly up to the castle, but nearly ran away when a giantess opened the door.

"You are just the lad I need to help me in the house," she grinned. "I will help you so that my husband will not find you and make a meal of you!"

The giantess thrust Jack into a wardrobe in the hall and then set about getting her husband's supper.

Jack heard a great voice.

"Fe-fa-fi-fo-fum, I smell the breath of an Englishman.
 Let him be alive or let him be dead,
 I'll grind his bones to make my bread."

"Sit down and eat this elephant stew," said his wife. "That is what you can smell."

The giant ate a huge meal and at once fell asleep. When he was snoring the giantess opened the door and let Jack out to help her. She pushed him back again when the giant wakened up and Jack pressed his eye against the keyhole to see what would happen.

"Bring me my little hen!"
roared the giant.

The giantess carried in a small brown hen and put it on the table in front of her husband.

"Lay!" he growled. The little brown hen laid two beautiful golden eggs. The giant dozed off and Jack pushed open the door and crept across to the table. He snatched up the little hen and ran away as fast as he could, and hurried down the beanstalk to the safety of his own little home.

Jack's mother wept for joy when she saw him, and when she heard the story of the old lady, she told Jack that it was all true.

"I will go back for other riches and the talking harp," cried Jack.

Jack's mother did not want him to go, but after a good night's sleep Jack climbed up the stout stems and stepped off into the same green countryside.

Jack hoped the giantess would take him on again as her servant, and as she did not have good eyesight and did not recognise the boy who had stolen her husband's hen, she agreed to let him come in and help her.

Everything happened as before, but this time it was his money bags the giant ordered to have brought to him. As soon as he slept Jack crept off with as many of them as he could carry and got them safely down the beanstalk.

"We shall never want again," cried his mother.

But Jack wanted his father's talking harp and the next day he climbed the beanstalk yet again.

Once more Jack managed to persuade the giantess to let him come in to help her, and again she hid him in the wardrobe when her husband came in.

"Fe-fa-fi-fo-fum, I smell the breath of an Englishman,
Let him be alive or let him be dead,
I'll grind his bones to make my bread," he roared.

"It's the lamb stew you can smell," the giantess told him. Eat it up." Which, of course, he did.

"Bring me my harp," he demanded.

The giantess brought the beautiful golden harp and put it on the table before the giant. Then it played to him until he fell asleep.

Jack crept out, snatched up the harp and ran away. But the harp did not like this.

"Master, master!" it cried.

At once the giant wakened and ran after Jack so fast that the boy only just got down the beanstalk in time. The giant began to climb down after him.

"Quickly, Mother, bring me an axe!" cried Jack.

His mother pushed the axe into her son's hand and with sure strokes he felled the great beanstalk.

Down it fell and with it came the giant, which was the end of him.

Later, Jack and his mother made the long journey back to the green countryside on the high cliff which the beanstalk had reached, and went to live in their own beautiful castle.

THE FROG PRINCE

IN the olden days there lived a King whose daughters were all beautiful, but the youngest of them was even lovelier than the others.

Near the castle of this King was a large and gloomy forest, and in the middle of the forest grew a very old tree, beneath whose branches splashed a little fountain.

Whenever the days were very warm, the youngest Princess went into the forest and sat down by the side of the fountain.

Her favourite plaything was a golden ball and she would throw it high into the air, and catch it as it came down again.

One sunny day the Princess rested by the fountain, as usual. She tossed the golden ball into the air, but this time she did not catch it and it rolled into the water.

The well beneath the fountain was very deep and the ball disappeared from sight and seemed gone for ever. The Princess began to cry and as she wept a voice called out to her.

"Why are you crying, dear Princess?" it asked.

The Princess looked everywhere to find who was speaking to her and at last she saw it was a big frog sitting on the side of the fountain.

The Princess was very surprised to hear a frog speak, and she replied at once.

"I did not catch my beautiful golden ball and it fell into the water," she said.

"Do not cry," said the frog. "I will help you if I can. What will you give me if I bring back the golden ball to you?"

"What would you like, dear frog?" said the Princess. "My dresses, my pearls and jewels, or my golden crown?"

"I cannot wear any of those things, little Princess," croaked the frog. "I would like you to take care of me and be my friend. I would like to eat from your plate and sleep in your bed. If you will promise me these things I will dive into the water and bring up your golden ball."

"I will promise anything you ask if only you will find the golden ball," cried the Princess.

The frog disappeared under the water. The Princess felt a little uneasy as she thought about her promise, but she did not think that she would have to carry it out.

Then the frog appeared again and this time he had in his large mouth the Princess's golden ball.

"Thank you very much, dear Frog!" she cried. She took it from him and began to run back to the castle.

"Wait for me! I cannot run as fast as you can!" cried the frog. "Remember your promise!"

But the louder he croaked the faster ran the ungrateful Princess.

The next day the King and his daughters were sitting at the table enjoying their lunch when they heard a strange sound.

Flip-flop splashetty! it went; all the way up the marble stairs and ending outside the door of the Banqueting Hall. Then came a knock at the door and a croaking voice was heard.

"Let me in!" it cried. "Open the door, youngest daughter of the King, and let me in!"

The little Princess went and opened the door and when she saw who was sitting outside she closed it quickly and went and sat down again, looking very pale.

"What is the matter?" asked the King. "You look as if a giant had come to carry you away."

"It is not a giant," wailed the Princess. "It is a great ugly old frog."

"What can a frog be doing here?" asked the King, in surprise.

"It is my own fault," said the Princess, tearfully. "He fetched my golden ball from the bottom of the fountain but first made me promise to let him come here and be my friend."

"He sounds a very unusual kind of frog," said the King. "But if you made a promise you must keep it. Let the frog in."

The frog hopped up to the Princess's chair.

"Let me sit on your chair, Princess," he croaked.

The Princess had to lift him up and put him beside her on the chair and from there he jumped on to the table.

"Now push your plate towards me so that we can share the same food," he croaked.

The Princess did so and the frog made a good meal.

"I have had enough to eat," said the frog. "Now I am tired and ready to go to sleep in your little bed."

The Princess burst into tears. She did not want a cold muddy frog in her bed. But the King was angry.

"The frog helped you when you needed him," he said. "You must not despise him now."

So the Princess had to carry the frog up to her room, but she laid him in a corner of the room. He soon jumped away from there.

"I want to sleep in your comfortable bed or I will tell your father," he croaked, unkindly.

At that the Princess was so cross that she picked up the poor frog and threw him across the room.

"Be quiet, you ugly old frog!" she cried.

But as he fell the poor frog changed into a handsome young Prince with a face and form not at all like that of a frog.

"I was bewitched and I had to stay in the shape of a frog until a kind Princess became my true friend," he told her.

"I was not kind," said the Princess, feeling ashamed.

But the Prince already loved her very much indeed and that was why they married and lived happily ever afterwards.

THE PRINCESS AND THE PEA

ONCE upon a time there was a handsome Prince who lived in a faraway land with his father and mother, the King and Queen of that country.

The Prince was anxious to marry, but he told his parents that his bride *must* be a Princess.

"Of course you must marry a Princess," agreed the King. "There are plenty to choose from. You have only to go and find the one you like best."

The King and Queen did not think their son would have much difficulty in finding a *real* Princess and they waved him happily on his way to find his future wife.

A few days later the Prince came back again, without a Princess.

"The one I went to see was not a *real* princess!" he sighed.

A week or so after that the Prince set off again. This time his parents were sure that the lovely princess he went to see would win his heart, but he came back without her.

"She was not a *real* princess!" he cried.

The King and Queen began to despair of their son ever finding a wife.

One night a dreadful storm blew up and in the middle of it there came a loud knocking at the oak door leading into the great hall. The King himself opened it and there, standing in the pouring rain, was a very beautiful girl.

Her clothes were dripping wet and her shoes were soaking. Her hair was hanging straight around her pale face and she was shivering with cold. "I am a Princess," she cried. "My carriage has broken down. My servants have scattered and I have lost them. Will you be so good as to let me have shelter for the night?"

"Are you a *real* Princess?" asked the Prince, looking at her doubtfully.

"Of course I am," said the girl, proudly.

"She does not look like a Princess," thought the Queen. "But I know how we can find out if she is telling the truth." And she went into the bedroom which was being prepared for the unexpected guest. She took the clothes from the bed and placed one little dried pea upon the mattress, then she sent for twenty more mattresses and ordered them to be placed over the pea. Not content with that she had some soft feather beds placed on top of the twenty mattresses. And that was where the Princess slept that night.

The next morning the Queen asked the guest how she had slept.

"Very badly indeed!" groaned the young lady. "I hardly had a wink of sleep all night. I was lying on something so hard that I must be black and blue all over."

At that the Queen smiled happily. "Here at last is your *real* Princess," she whispered to her son. "Nobody but a *real* Princess could have such a tender skin as that!"

The Prince, who had fallen in love with her the night before, begged her to marry him, and the Princess liked the Prince so much that she was pleased to marry him and so they lived happily ever afterwards.